To Sally, with love – R S

To Mark, from a grateful Dad – M T

LITTLE TIGER PRESS
1 The Coda Centre, 189 Munster Road, London SW6 6AW
www.littletiger.co.uk

First published in Great Britain 2006
This edition published 2016

Text copyright © Ragnhild Scamell 2006
Illustrations copyright © Michael Terry 2006
Ragnhild Scamell and Michael Terry have asserted
their rights to be identified as the author and
illustrator of this work under the Copyright,
Designs and Patents Act, 1988

Printed in China • LTP/1800/1726/1016

10 9 8 7 6 5 4 3 2 1

Ragnhild Scamell

Illustrated by

Michael Terry

ouch!

LITTLE TIGER PRESS
London

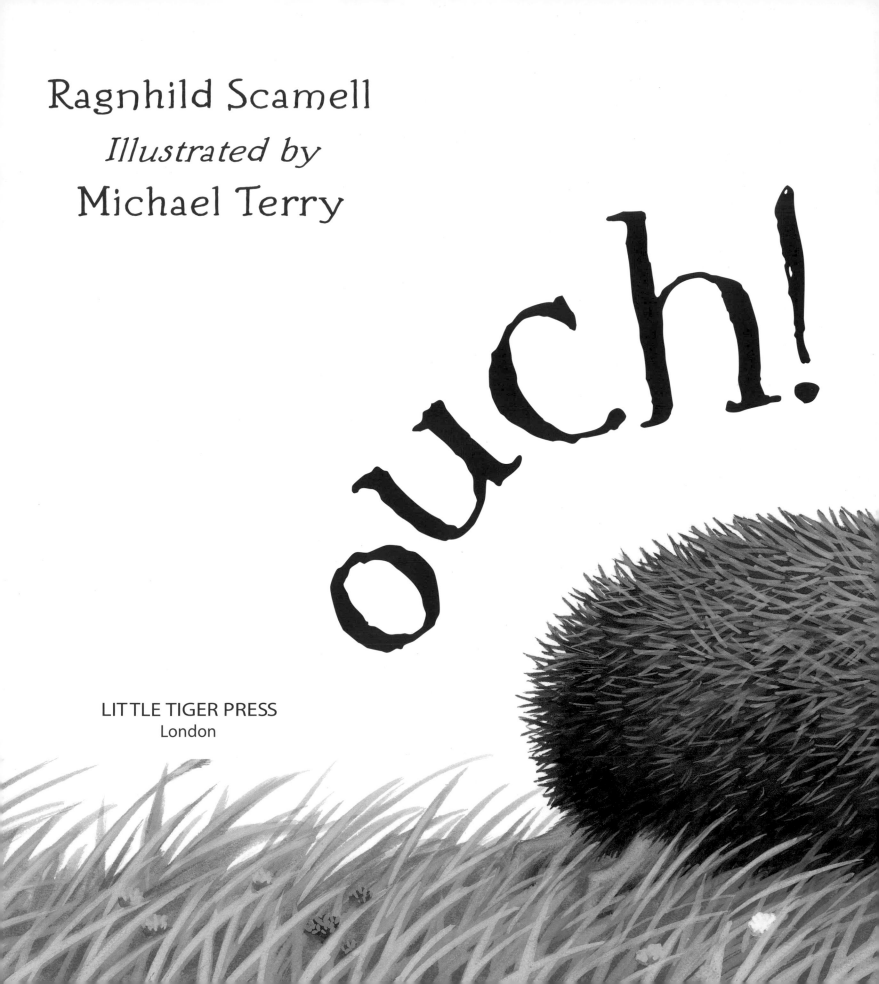

Hedgehog had just finished building her winter nest under the old apple tree. Not too large and not too small. Just right for a nice long winter sleep.

Suddenly a juicy red apple landed on her back. "Ouch!" squeaked Hedgehog.

Plop!

She curled into a spiny ball, hoping it would fall off. But when she uncurled, the juicy red apple was still there.

Hedgehog tried to squeeze herself and the apple into the beautiful new nest. But could she get in? No. She could not. Not with the apple on her back. The nest was too small.

Oh dear!

Squirrel, scurrying past with an armful of brown nuts, stopped to help.

"Stand still. I'll push the apple off," he said.

And he pushed. And he struggled.

And he heaved. And he tugged . . .

But the juicy red apple stayed where it was. Worse still, three of Squirrel's brown nuts got caught in Hedgehog's spines. So now she had a juicy red apple and three brown nuts on her back.

"Oh dear!" wailed Hedgehog. "Winter is coming and I can't get into my nest. What will I do?"
"Try rolling on your back," snorted Pig, trotting up. "That'll get rid of it all."

Hedgehog threw herself
on the ground. Her little
legs paddled in the air as
she twisted and wriggled
and rolled.

"Has it all gone?" she asked hopefully,
scrabbling to her feet.

Pig shook his head. No. The juicy
red apple and the three brown nuts
were still there. So were a small green
pear and a crumpled brown leaf.

"Oh dear," sighed Hedgehog,
rolling her eyes.

But up in the sky,
sailing towards Hedgehog,
she saw a colourful bit
of card.

"Bother!" she cried.
This way and that she ran,
as fast as she could.

This way and that drifted
the card . . .

. . . and landed right on her back, between the apple and the three brown nuts.

"It's not fair!" cried Hedgehog, who now had a juicy red apple, three brown nuts, a small green pear, a crumpled brown leaf and a colourful bit of card on her back. "I'll never get into my nest!"

Hedgehog pattered to the pond and gazed at her reflection in the water. "Hello, Hedgehog. That's a lot of stuff on your back," croaked Frog. "Hmph! I'm trying to get rid of it," sniffed Hedgehog. "Dive," said Frog. "That will wash it off."

Hedgehog dipped a foot in the murky water, then dived.

Splash! Her friends watched Hedgehog bobbing up and down. The juicy red apple, the three brown nuts, the small green pear, the crumpled brown leaf and the colourful bit of card were all still there. So was a pink water lily.

"Glug-glug-glug," gurgled Hedgehog
as the others heaved her out of the
water. She did look funny!

But Hedgehog did not find it funny.
"Stop laughing!" she spluttered and
stamped her feet on the ground.
"Where am I going to sleep?"
Pig and Squirrel looked worried.
So did Frog.

"I do have one last idea," oinked Pig. "Squeeze through that hedge over there. That'll brush everything off."

So Hedgehog closed her eyes and squeezed herself through the thick leaves. But did it get everything off her back?

No. It did not. It was all still there.
So were four ripe blackberries.
And staring at her, with a look
of great surprise, stood Goat!

"Oooh!" cried Goat. "You've brought LUNCH!"

"Help yourself," said Hedgehog. "Take it all."

"Yippee!" brayed Goat. Then he picked off and ate the juicy red apple, the three brown nuts, the small green pear, the pink water lily and the four ripe blackberries. For pudding, he ate the card. The only thing he left was the crumpled brown leaf. He just couldn't eat any more.

"Hoorah!" cried Hedgehog. She felt as light as a feather. "Thank you, Goat," she said.

Then she ran, as fast as her little legs could carry her, through the gate, past the pond, across the orchard, under the tree and home to her nest.

Hedgehog squeezed into her little nest. It fitted her perfectly. And it was the best nest ever. Outside a cold wind blew another apple off the tree.

But it didn't fall on
Hedgehog. She was
safe in her nest and
fast, fast asleep.

More fabulous books from Little Tiger Press!

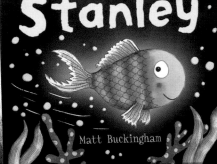

Bright Stanley

Matt Buckingham

Bored Bill

Liz Pichon

Rhino's Great BIG Itch!

Natalie Chivers

OUCh!

Ragnhild Scamell · Michael Terry

THE BIGGEST BADDEST WOLF

Nick Ward

A Little Fairy Magic

Julia Hubery · Alison Edgson

For information regarding any of the above titles
or for our catalogue, please contact us:
Little Tiger Press, 1 The Coda Centre, 189 Munster Road, London SW6 6AW
Tel: 020 7385 6333 • E-mail: contact@littletiger.co.uk • www.littletiger.co.uk